828 I Street
Sacramento, CA 95814
08/19

KHALID

by Emily Hudd

CAPSTONE PRESS
a capstone imprint

Bright Idea Books are published by Capstone Press
1710 Roe Crest Drive, North Mankato, Minnesota 56003
www.mycapstone.com

Copyright © 2020 by Capstone Press, a Capstone imprint. All rights reserved. No part of this publication may be reproduced in whole or in part, or stored in a retrieval system, or transmitted in any form or by any means, electronic, mechanical, photocopying, recording, or otherwise, without written permission of the publisher.

Library of Congress Cataloging-in-Publication Data
Names: Hudd, Emily.
Title: Khalid / by Emily Hudd.
Description: North Mankato, Minnesota : Capstone Press, [2020] | Series: Influential people | Includes index.
Identifiers: LCCN 2018060992 (print) | LCCN 2018061246 (ebook) | ISBN 9781543571493 (ebook) | ISBN 9781543571387 (hardcover)
Subjects: LCSH: Khalid, 1998- --Juvenile literature. | Singers--United States--Juvenile literature.
Classification: LCC ML3930.K43 (ebook) | LCC ML3930.K43 H84 2020 (print) | DDC 782.42164092 [B] --dc23
LC record available at https://lccn.loc.gov/2018060992

All internet sites appearing in back matter were available and accurate when this book was sent to press.

Editorial Credits
Editor: Claire Vanden Branden
Designer: Becky Daum
Production Specialist: Melissa Martin

Photo Credits
Alamy: Daniel DeSlover/ZUMA Press, Inc./Alamy Live News, 10–11; Kim M. Leland/Gonzales Photo/Alamy Live News, 16–17; Samy Khabthani/Gonzales Photo, 26–27; AP Images: Jordan Strauss/Invision, cover; Newscom: PG/Splash News, 22; Rex Features: 21, Steven Ferdman, 15; Shutterstock Images: agwilson, 25, Ben Houdijk, 5, 28, Kathy Hutchins, 7, 13, 18–19, 31, leoks/Shutterstock Images, 9

Design Elements: Shutterstock Images

```
Printed in the United States of America.
PA70
```

TABLE OF CONTENTS

CHAPTER ONE
A NEW STAR 4

CHAPTER TWO
EARLY LIFE 8

CHAPTER THREE
RISE TO FAME 14

CHAPTER FOUR
MAKING IT BIG 20

Glossary 28
Timeline 29
Activity 30
Further Resources 32
Index 32

CHAPTER 1

A NEW Star

Fans waited with excitement. Then they started to scream. Khalid was walking on stage. He began to sing his song "American Teen." He pointed at them and smiled. People sang along.

Khalid was on his first music **tour**. It lasted from July to September in 2017. Khalid traveled across the United States. He had 25 shows. The tour was for his first **album**, *American Teen*. It had come out earlier that year.

Khalid enjoys dancing during his performances.

THE GRAMMYS

Khalid was **nominated** five times for the 60th **Grammy Awards**. One was for Song of the Year. Khalid worked with the artist Logic. They made the song "1-800-273-8255." The song was about people who deal with hard times. Many people loved it.

Khalid's music journey had just started. In 2016 he was a high school student. By 2017 he was a famous singer.

Khalid did not win a Grammy Award in 2018, but he has won many other awards.

CHAPTER 2

EARLY Life

Khalid Robinson was born February 11, 1998. His father died when Khalid was young. His mother was in the **military**. Khalid moved a lot as a child. He lived in Germany for six years. He also spent four years living in New York.

Khalid became interested in music when he was 3 years old. His mother sang around the house. His family listened to music while he was growing up.

Khalid lived in Heidelberg, Germany, for a while when he was young.

Khalid's music has been inspired by his experiences growing up.

THE MOVE

In 2015 Khalid and his family moved to El Paso, Texas. He was 17 years old. It was not easy to move. He missed his friends in New York. He wrote music to help him through this time.

Khalid spent his free time recording songs. He later said moving to Texas turned out great. Khalid met new people. He had new song ideas.

Khalid took his emotions and turned them into song lyrics.

CHAPTER 3

RISE TO Fame

Khalid was a senior in high school in 2016. He started posting songs to SoundCloud. SoundCloud is a music sharing website.

His music spread. People loved it.

Then Khalid went to a recording studio.

He made the song "Location."

Khalid thought he would grow up to be a music teacher before he became famous.

People listened to "Location" on their phones. They shared it with friends. Khalid graduated from high school in May 2016. That same day television star Kylie Jenner listened to the song. She posted about it on her social media. Then the song became very popular. Khalid's life changed forever.

"LOCATION"

"Location" has more than 380 million views on YouTube. It has been listened to more than 89 million times on SoundCloud.

Khalid soon began singing in front of thousands of people.

Khalid is inspired by many different kinds of music.

FIRST ALBUM

The music company RCA Records saw Khalid's talent. They helped him make *American Teen*. It came out March 3, 2017. It was number nine on **Billboard**'s top 200 albums list. It sold more than 1 million copies.

CHAPTER 4

MAKING It Big

Many people started to notice Khalid. They wanted to work with him. He was young and fresh. He could sing many types of music.

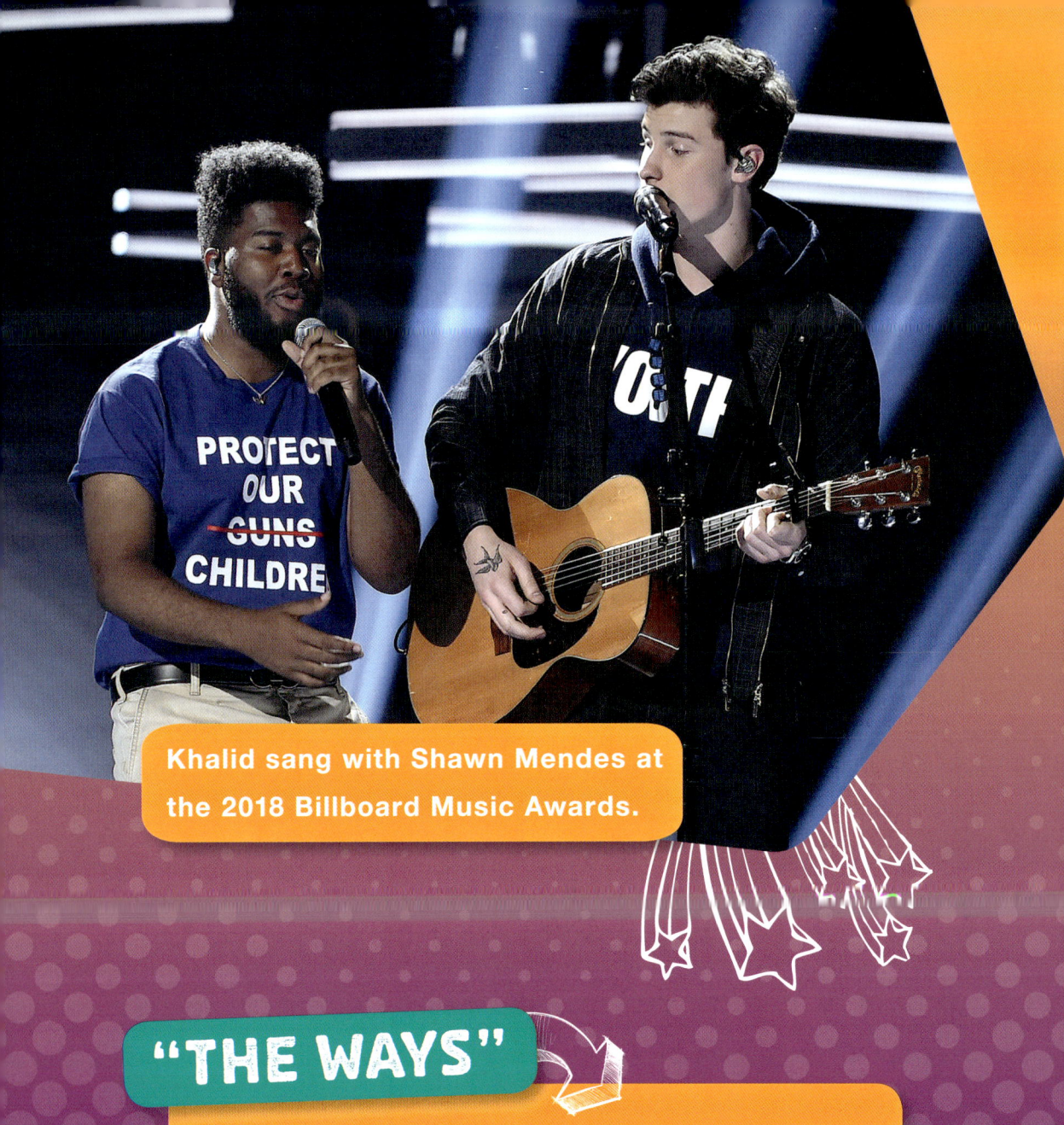

Khalid sang with Shawn Mendes at the 2018 Billboard Music Awards.

"THE WAYS"

Khalid and Swae Lee recorded "The Ways" together. It was in the movie *Black Panther*.

WORKING WITH OTHER ARTISTS

Khalid worked with many artists in 2018. He sang with rapper Kendrick Lamar. He worked with young artists like Shawn Mendes. Some of his songs were in movies.

Khalid also worked with singer Normani. They made the song "Love Lies." It came out in February 2018. It has been listened to more than 500 million times on Spotify. It was also in the movie *Love, Simon*.

SECOND ALBUM

Khalid made his second album in 2018. It was called *Suncity*. It had seven songs. One is in Spanish. *Suncity* was Billboard's top **R&B** album in November 2018.

Khalid promoted his new album, *Suncity*, in 2018.

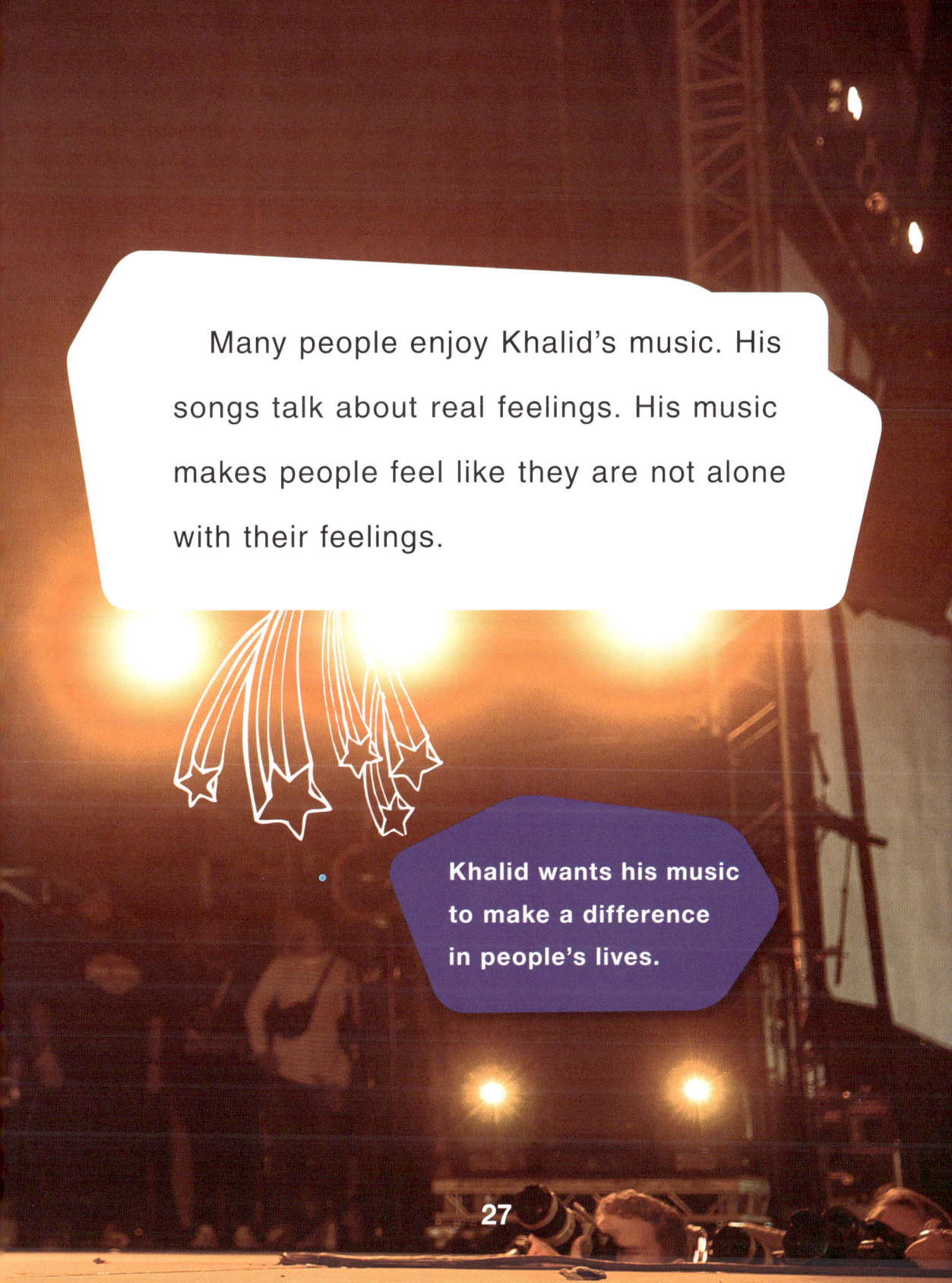

Many people enjoy Khalid's music. His songs talk about real feelings. His music makes people feel like they are not alone with their feelings.

Khalid wants his music to make a difference in people's lives.

GLOSSARY

album
a collection of songs

Billboard
a music company that ranks songs and artists

Grammy Award
an award that honors the best artists in music

military
part of the United States armed forces

nominate
to suggest that a person might be the right one for a job or an award

R&B
popular music usually including parts of blues and African American folk music and marked by a strong beat and simple chords

tour
a number of shows performed in a row

TIMELINE

1998: Khalid Robinson is born on February 11.

2015: Khalid moves to El Paso, Texas.

2016: Khalid graduates high school. On the same day, Kylie Jenner puts "Location" on her Snapchat.

2017: Khalid releases his first album, *American Teen*.

2017: Khalid goes on tour.

2017: Khalid is nominated for five Grammys.

2018: Khalid makes his second album, *Suncity*.

ACTIVITY

WRITE YOUR OWN SONG

Khalid writes about things that happen in his life. He takes his feelings and turns them into music. Take a few minutes to think about something big that has happened in your life. How did it make you feel? Write down your experience. Now turn those feelings into a song! Don't forget to give your song a title.

FURTHER RESOURCES

**Ready to learn more about music?
Check out these resources:**

Anniss, Matthew. *Create Your Own Music*. Media Genius. North Mankato, Minn.: Heinemann-Raintree, 2017.

DK Find Out!: World Music Day
https://www.dkfindout.com/us/more-find-out/special-events/world-music-day

Walker, Carolina. *You Can Work in Music*. You Can Work In the Arts. North Mankato, Minn.: Capstone Press, 2019.

**Want to learn more about other artists?
Take a look at this resource:**

London, Martha. *Kendrick Lamar*. Influential People. North Mankato, Minn.: Capstone Press, 2020.

INDEX

"1-800-273-8255," 6

American Teen, 5, 19

Black Panther, 22

El Paso, Texas, 11

Grammy Awards, 6

Jenner, Kylie, 16

Lamar, Kendrick, 23
"Location," 15–16
Love, Simon, 23

Mendes, Shawn, 23

New York, 8, 11
Normani, 23

RCA Records, 19

SoundCloud, 14, 16
Spotify, 23
Suncity, 24

tour, 5